Amadeus

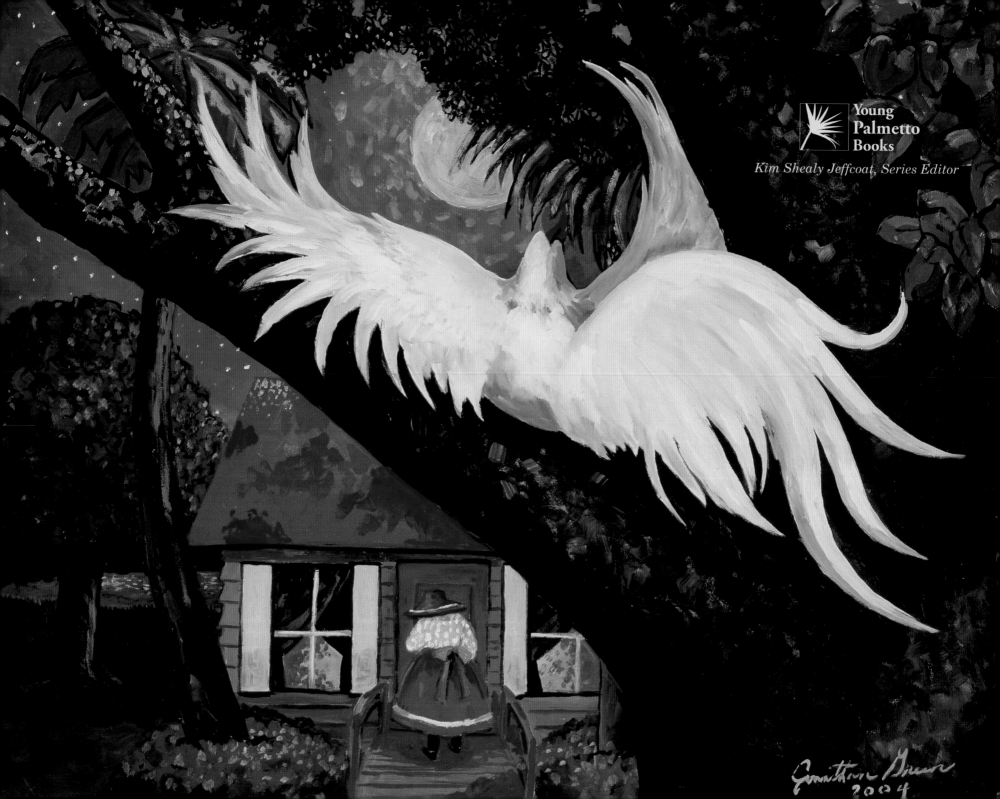

Young
Palmetto
Books

Kim Shealy Jeffcoat, Series Editor

Amadeus
The Leghorn Rooster

Delores B. Nevils

Illustrated by Jonathan Green

The University of South Carolina Press

On the island of St. Helena, South Carolina, there is a widow lady who lives in a tiny cottage that has twenty-six windows. A ramp, painted red, leads to the doorway.

Clusters of pink and red azaleas and yellow forsythia line the circular drive. In the springtime, the widow lady's yard is a wonderland of pretty colors.

Palmetto trees, South Carolina's state tree, surround the cottage. From the many windows, the widow lady watches the tall palmettos bow and sway, bow and sway, when strong winds blow in from the Atlantic Ocean. The trees wave to passersby, inviting them to come into the tiny cottage for a visit.

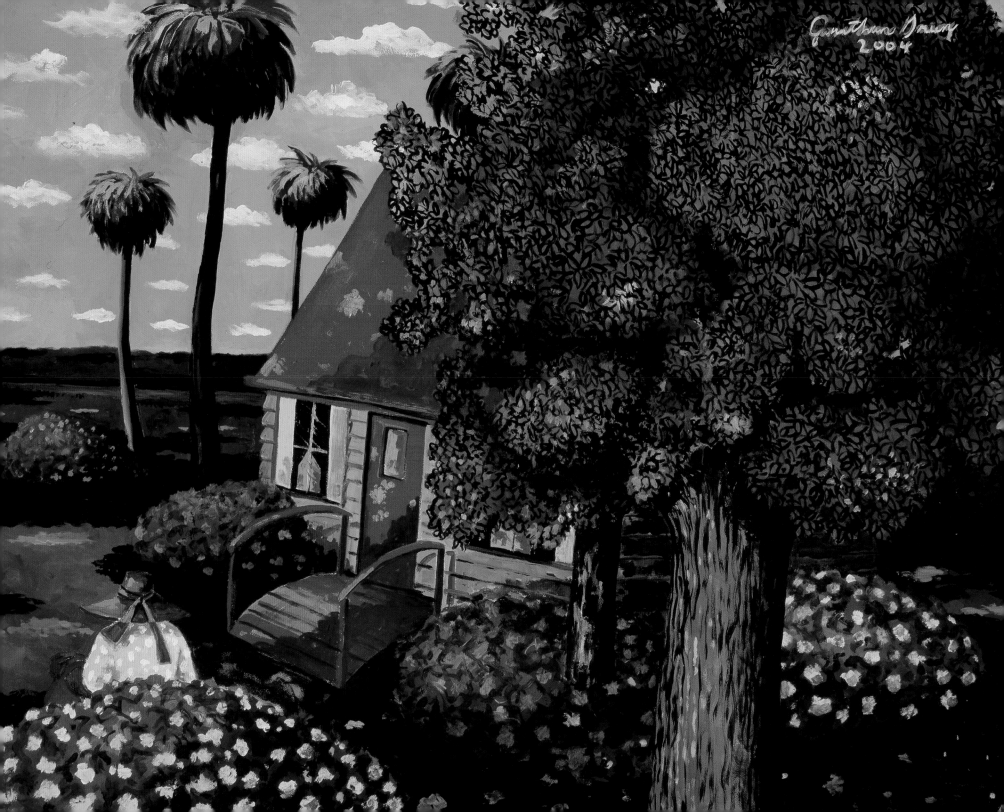

Two kittens, a mother cat, and two dogs came to live with the widow lady.

Scooter was a gray and white kitten. Pumpkin was white and orange—the color is how she got her name. Mae Liza, the mama cat, was gray striped with four white paws that looked like little shoes.

The cats did not live in the tiny cottage. They lived outside where they could run and play. When the weather turned cold, the cats scampered under the house and burrowed in leaves. Snuggled together, they kept cozy and warm.

Whenever the widow lady was in her yard,

Mae Liza walked close to her, purring and purring. The mother cat knew Scooter and Pumpkin loved the widow lady very much.

The dogs were named Kane and Able. Kane was golden brown with white spots on his neck and ears. He was big, weighing about a hundred pounds. Able was Kane's brother. He was smaller, but his fur was the same color.

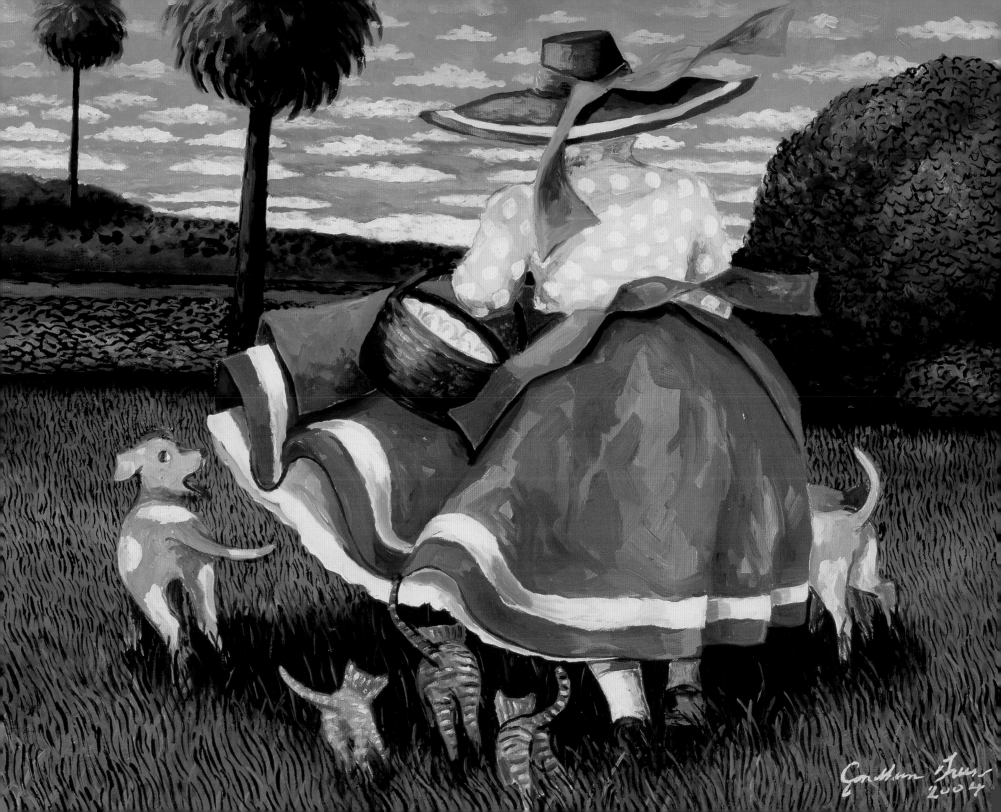

The widow lady had a special reason for giving the dogs their names. Kane was sometimes mean, and he growled at anyone who came close to him. Able always wagged his tail when people came near, eager for a pat on his head or a scratch behind his ears.

Kane and Able played with the mother cat and kittens. The dogs would never hurt the kittens because they knew the widow lady loved all of them. The five playmates were happy living at the tiny island cottage.

Early one morning, the widow lady was awakened by a "COCK-A-DOODLE-DOO! COCK-A-DOODLE-DOO!" She jumped out of bed and ran to the door.

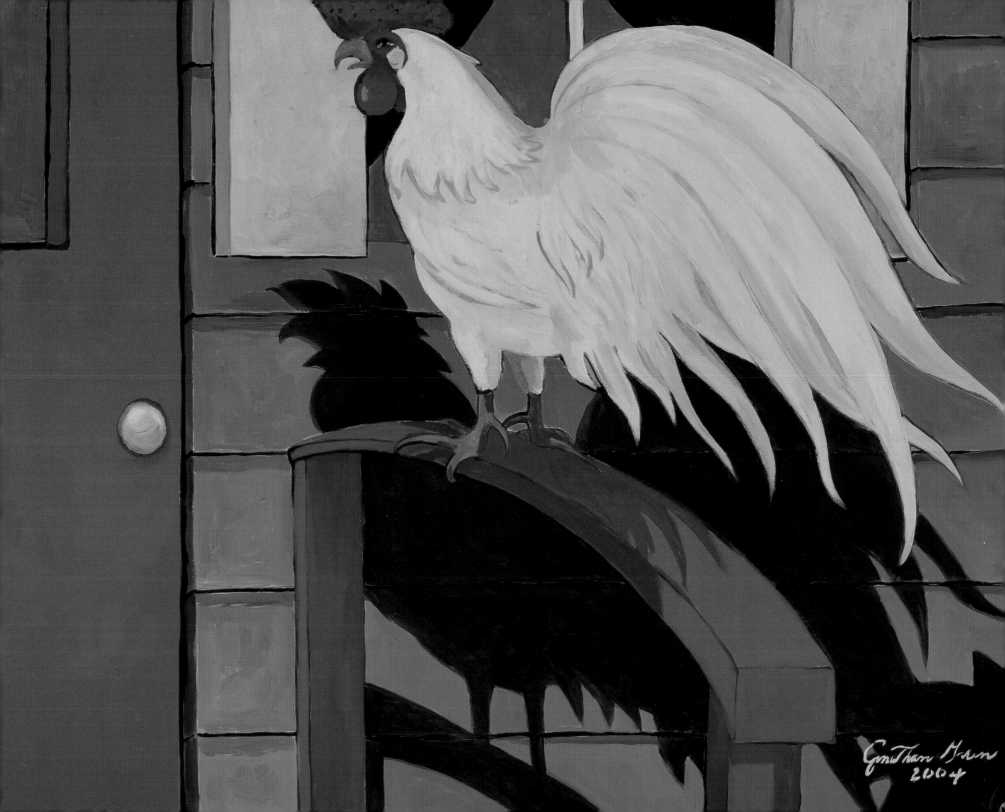

Standing in the open doorway, she rubbed her eyes in disbelief. There, on the red ramp, perched a white rooster— the most beautiful rooster she had ever seen. His long tail feathers stood tall and proud.

The widow lady knew this was no ordinary rooster. She went back inside and pulled a big book from her bookshelf.

This was no ordinary book. It had facts about almost everything in the world anybody wanted to know.

Lo and behold! Twenty roosters filled one entire page. Each rooster had a red crown on top of its head. But only one was covered in white feathers. This was a leghorn rooster.

For the next three weeks, the widow lady and the cats and dogs were awakened early each morning by "COCK-A-DOODLE-DOO!" The leghorn also crowed during the afternoon, wandering all around the yard. The widow lady ran after the rooster and tried to shoo him away. She chased him around and around the tiny cottage, but he would not leave.

After all the running, the widow lady grew very tired. She knew the beautiful leghorn rooster had made himself a home. Deep down, she was pleased he stayed. He was so beautiful!

"What shall I name this rooster?" she asked herself.

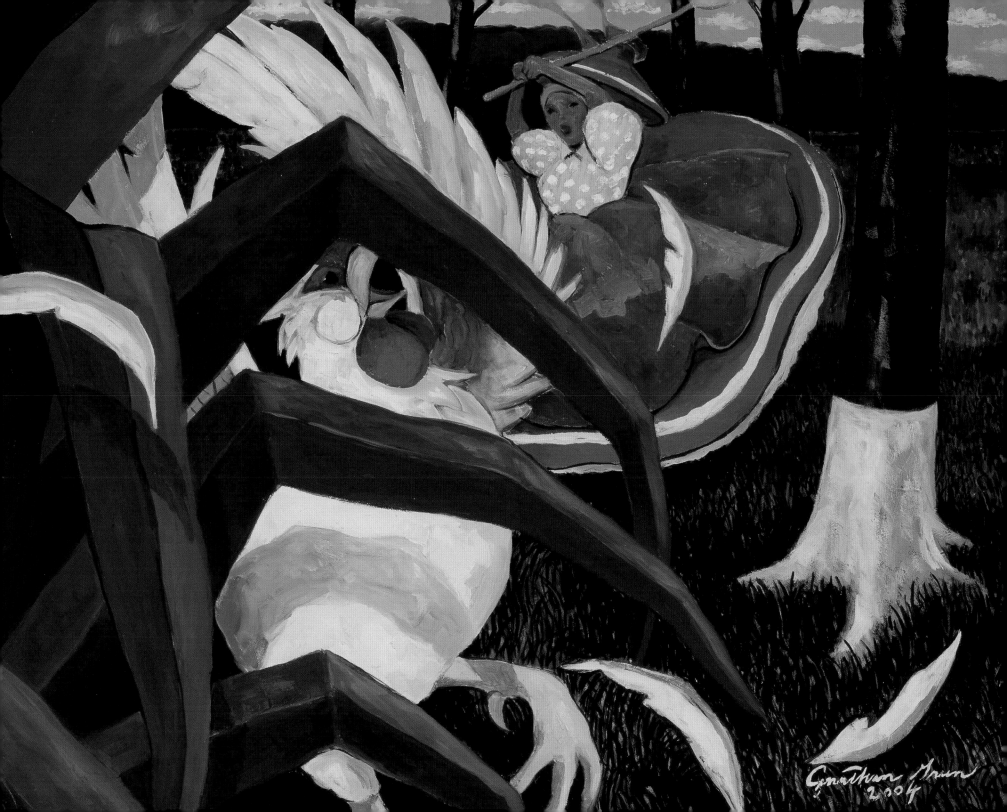

The following morning, about five o'clock, the widow lady awoke to the leghorn's "COCK-A-DOODLE-DOO!" She had watched him each afternoon as he strutted around the yard, crowing. He moved about with a skip or a hop, boastful with his high steps. He probably had a high opinion of himself.

His crowing and strutting had a special rhythm—like the music of Wolfgang Amadeus Mozart, a great classical composer who lived in the 1700s. If the rooster was going to stay, the widow lady decided, she would call him "Amadeus."

Amadeus wasted no time letting the other
animals know he was the boss of the yard.

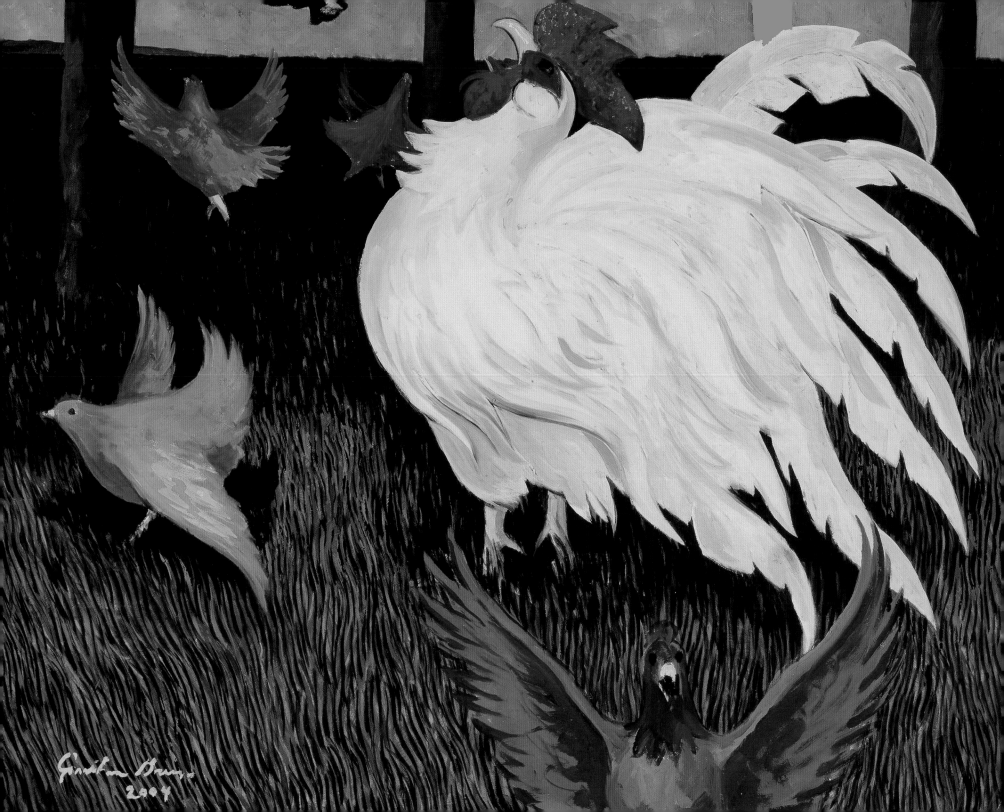

He flew up into an old live oak tree. Perched on a dark limb, he had a great view of the yard below, with its thousands of colorful wildflowers. From atop the oak, he could also survey the yard around the tiny cottage and see what the cats and dogs were doing. He decided to make his bed in that tree.

Around dawn each day, Amadeus announced to the widow lady, Kane, Able, Mae Liza, Scooter, and Pumpkin that he was awake. In fact, his "COCK-A-DOODLE-DOO!" was heard throughout the small Corners community of St. Helena.

Watching Amadeus strut and peck around the yard gave the widow lady such pleasure. She threw out corn for him to eat, but he was picky and would not eat it. One day she tossed a stale Kaiser roll outside. To her surprise, Amadeus pecked away at it. *"How outrageous!"* she thought. But every week, on her trip to the supermarket, she bought Kaiser rolls just for her beautiful leghorn rooster.

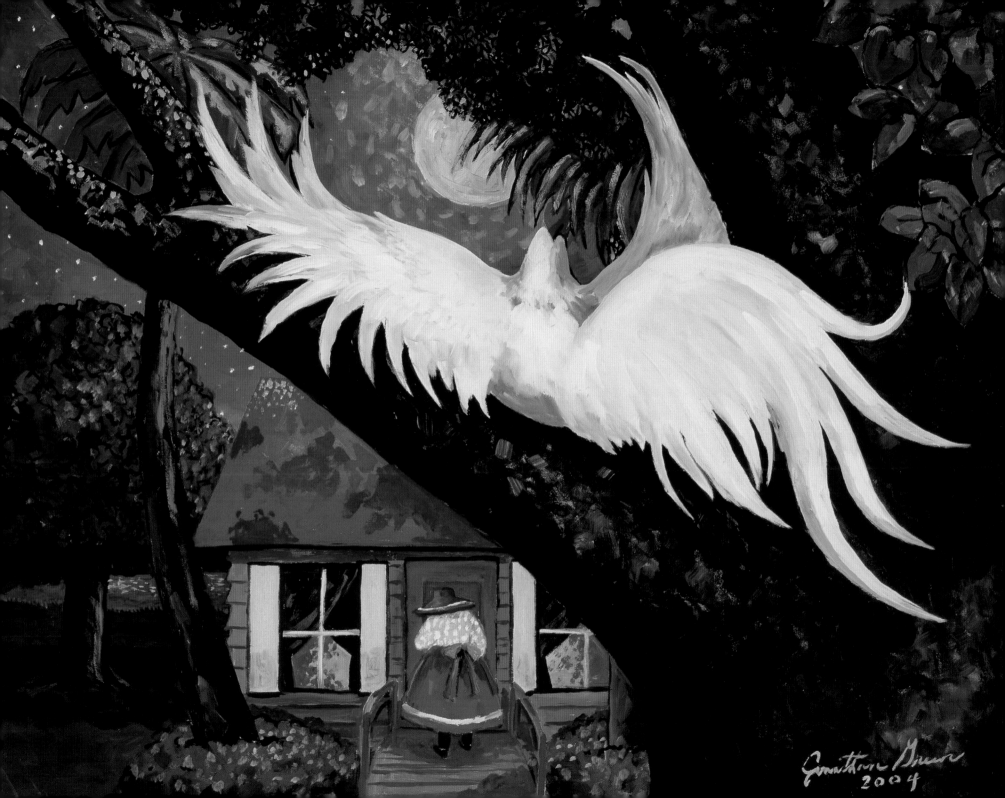

Amadeus annoyed Scooter and Pumpkin, waking them so early in the morning. The kittens rubbed their eyes with their little paws and complained, "Why does he have to wake us so early? We don't get any sleep anymore."

Cuddling her kittens, Mae Liza gave them their morning baths. *"Oh, dear, oh dear,"* she thought, *"the widow lady has given Amadeus too much freedom around here."*

Amadeus loved to perch on the railing of the red ramp and "COCK-A-DOODLE-DOO!" It didn't matter whether it was morning or afternoon.

Visitors came from near and far to see Amadeus. A minister from Romania, a small eastern European country, and a minister from Kansas City, Missouri, came. How delighted they were to see such a majestic rooster. He was a favorite of all the children in the community.

One day, the widow lady was in the washroom of her tiny cottage when she heard a knock at the door. "Just a minute," she said. "I'll be right there."

The visitor knocked again . . . and again.

The knocking grew louder.

Walking toward the door, the widow lady called, "Just a minute, please."

She pulled open the door and there stood Amadeus. The widow lady threw her head back and laughed. She laughed so hard tears ran down her cheeks.

Amadeus perched on the railing of the red ramp and began to "COCK-A-DOODLE-DOO!" as loudly as he could.

Scooter and Pumpkin witnessed the whole scene. The widow lady sure did love the new rooster! "Does this mean Amadeus is the widow lady's favorite?" they wondered.

The kittens and mother cat huddled together on the north side of the yard. They were very displeased.

"We've got to get rid of Amadeus," Mae Liza exclaimed, "Just look at him all puffed up! Now the widow lady no longer loves us, but she adores him."

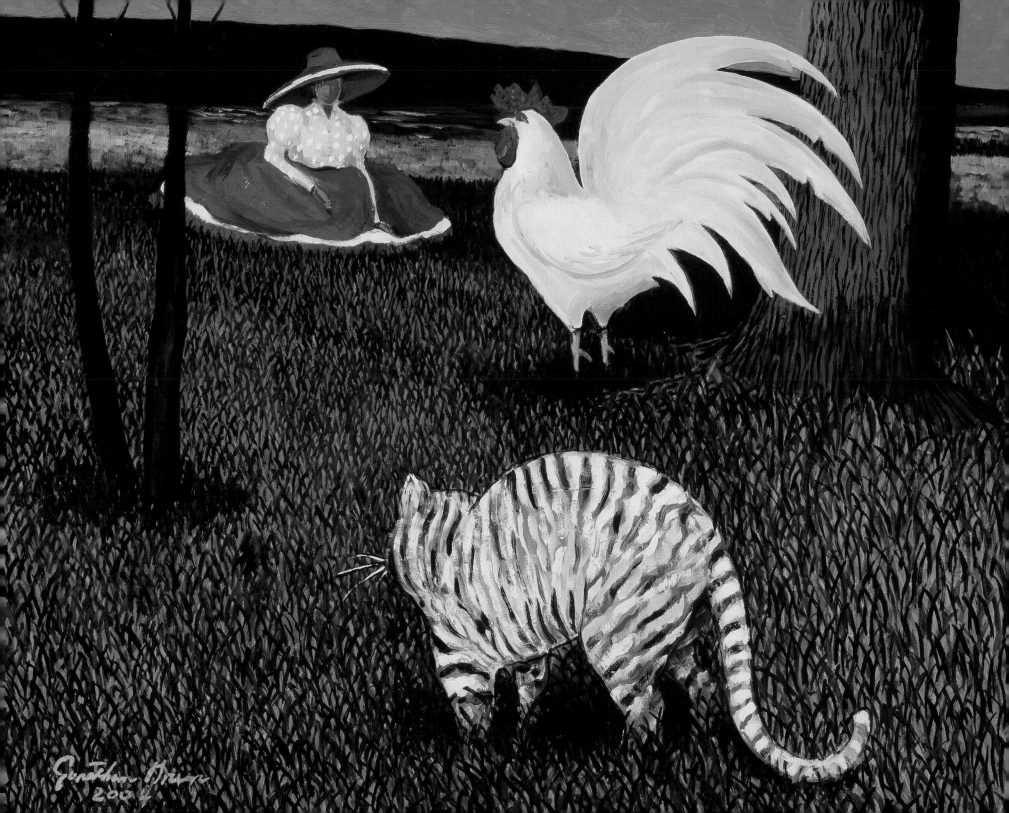

The three began to hatch a plan. "Here's how it will work," explained the mother cat. "We will scratch and scratch to start a hole where the dogs are chained. Kane and Able can pull loose from the post and chase Amadeus away."

The kittens and the mother cat knew Kane and Able were suspected of harming neighborhood chickens. Everybody on St. Helena talked about it. But the widow lady would not listen to that kind of talk.

The widow lady did not leave her dogs chained all the time. Every day she leashed Kane and Able and took them on a three-and-a-half-mile walk to and from the St. Helena post office. Neighbors watched and waved as the three walked by.

Early the next morning, to the cats' delight, Kane and Able pulled themselves loose. The widow lady was surprised to see the dogs run past her window. Looking out, she watched in horror as the dogs raced about, each holding a neighbors' chicken in his mouth. She called to the dogs, but they paid her no attention. Anyway, it was too late. They dogs settled down under a shade tree, proud of their catch. They did not know they had anything wrong.

They widow lady fell into a deep despair. She held her head in her hands and wept. She felt so sad for the poor chickens. But she knew if Kane and Able would hurt the neighbors' chickens, they might also hurt Amadeus.

Feeling she had no choice, the widow lady called the animal shelter and asked them to take the dogs away. "Maybe," she said, "someone will have a large fenced yard where they can play and stay out of trouble."

Scooter, Pumpkin, and Mae Liza were very sad. Their friends were gone, and Amadeus was still there. If the widow lady got rid of Kane and Able, they decided, she might also get rid of them. "She doesn't love us anymore," Mae Liza moaned. "And Amadeus is the boss of the yard. We must leave too."

After the kittens and mother cat left, Amadeus became lonely. He liked them and thought of the kittens as his playmates. Oftentimes people passing by the tiny cottage saw Amadeus pinning Mae Liza down with his feet on her back so she could not cuddle and play with her kittens. Amadeus thought Scooter and Pumpkin belonged to him.

Weeks passed. Amadeus spent his days wandering around the yard. His "cock-a-doodle-doo" began to sound weak, and he grew frail. He was so unhappy.

The widow lady was sad too. Her little cottage had once been joyful. One evening at dusk she looked up in the tall, dark oak tree to wish goodnight to Amadeus. But Amadeus was not there.

Days went by and Amadeus did not return. The widow lady began telling her friends that her prized rooster was missing. Her heart was broken.

Amadeus had left as suddenly as he appeared.

Today, the widow lady still lives in her tiny cottage. She misses her animal friends and remembers when her yard was filled with activity and play. To all who will listen, the widow lady tells the tale of Amadeus, the amazing leghorn rooster.

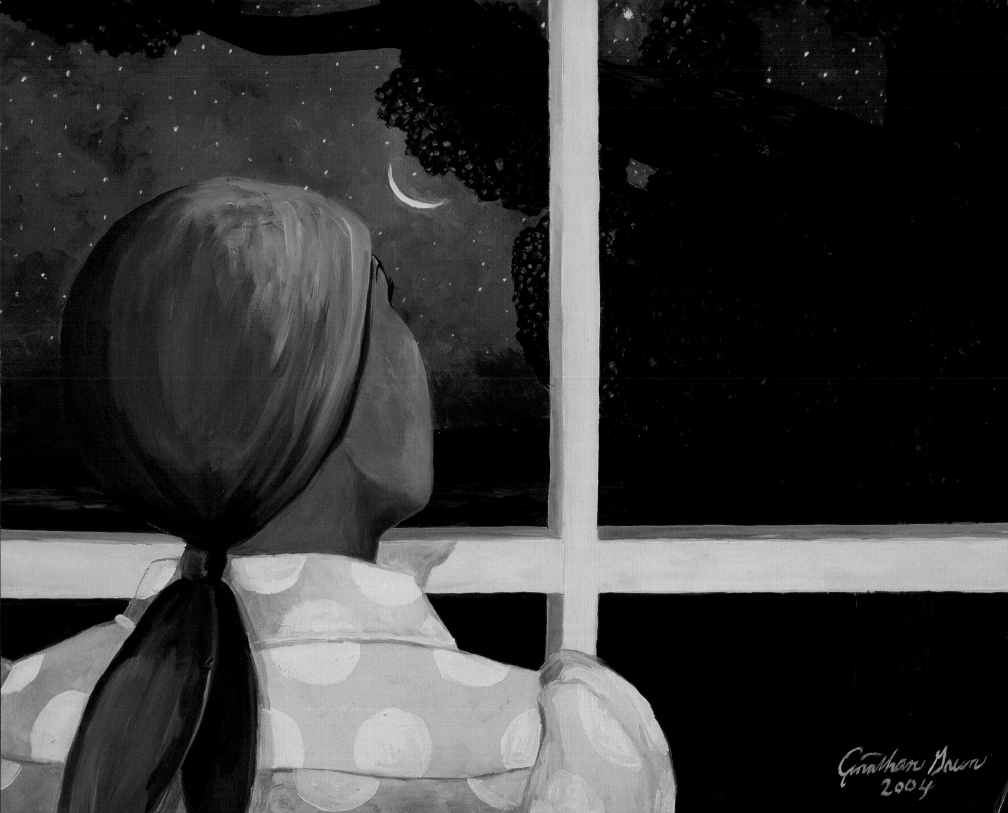

Dear Reader,

I've written this story down so that you too can know about Amadeus, the leghorn rooster of St. Helena Island. If you visit the South Carolina coast, please keep an eye out for him. Perhaps he went to live with Scooter and Pumpkin in their new home. Wherever he is, I hope he is happy.

Delores B. Nevils

Acknowledgments

I would like to acknowledge the support, assistance, and encouragement of the following: the Arts Council of Beaufort County, South Carolina; Jonathan Green, who loved my story and illustrated it with such brilliance; Amanda Gallman, Sandlapper Publishing Company, my first publisher; Barbara Stone, my first editor; Christine L Stanley, Bay Street Trading Company, Beaufort; Pam Coaxum, St. Helena Island, who inspired me to write the story; Mildred Warren, New York, who insisted I get the story published; Marie Ferguson, who cared for Amadeus when I was out of town; Nathalie Daise, Miss Nathalie's Workshop; Lynn Corliss, Brad Burnham, and Janet Dolly Nash, my strong supporters; Tommy L. Williams, Slidell, Louisiana, who had faith in my book; the University of South Carolina at Beaufort, for allowing me into the classroom to read my story; Marge Jarvis, Dataw Island, for inviting me to read the story of Amadeus at St. Helena Elementary School to first-graders who loved it and asked poignant questions; Ellen Zisholz, Alluette Jones Smalls, Susan Madison, and Jan Spencer, all of whom assisted me in many ways; George D. Kessler, regional coordinator, master tree farmer, Clemson Extension Service, for 2004; and the many unnamed folks of Beaufort County and elsewhere who gave me encouragement and moral support.

About the author

Delores B. Nevils, a Massachusetts native, was a member of the Art League of Manhattan and social secretary to the food editor for the *Ladies Home Journal* before moving to South Carolina in 1977. Nevils has been a newspaper columnist, a sign painter, a tree farmer, and a founding organizer of the Gullah Festival of South Carolina. She is also a contributing writer to *Seeking: Poetry and Prose Inspired by the Art of Jonathan Green*.

Text © 2016 Delores B. Nevils
Illustrations © 2016 Jonathan Green
First cloth edition, Sandlapper Publishing Inc., 2004

Published by the University of South Carolina Press
Columbia, South Carolina 29208

www.sc.edu/uscpress

Manufactured in Shenzhen, China

25 24 23 22 21 20 19 18 17 16   10 9 8 7 6 5 4 3 2 1

Library of Congress Cataloging-in-Publication Data can be
found at http://catalog.loc.gov/.

ISBN: 978-1-61117-556-1 (hardcover)
ISBN: 978-1-61117-557-8 (ebook)